VIKING
Published by the Penguin Group
Viking Penguin, a division of Penguin Books USA Inc.,
40 West 23rd Street, New York, New York, 10010, U.S.A.
Penguin Books Australia Ltd, Ringwood, Victoria, Australia
Penguin Books Canada Ltd, 2801 John Street, Markham, Ontario, Canada L3R 1B4
Penguin Books (N.Z.) Ltd, 182-190 Wairau Road, Auckland 10, New Zealand

First published in Great Britain by Aurum Books for Children, 1990

First American edition published in 1990

1 3 5 7 10 8 6 4 2

Library of Congress Catalogue Card Number: 89-51481.
ISBN: 0-670-83256-1

Printed in Great Britain

Mr. MacGregor's Breakfast Egg

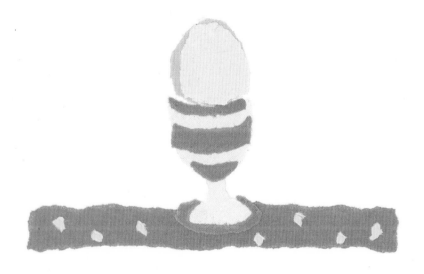

Story by Elizabeth MacDonald
Pictures by Alex Ayliffe

VIKING

EARLY ONE MORNING, Mother Duck and her ducklings
set off for a swim.

They were going to the pond down the road but,
when they reached the bottom of the hill, they
found Mr. Cameron's truck blocking their path.

"Quack! Quack!" said Mother Duck.

"Cheep! Cheep!" said the ducklings—
but the truck didn't move.

Mr. Cameron wanted to deliver some corn to
Mr. MacGregor, the farmer who lived on the hill,
but he couldn't—
because a herd of cattle was in his way.

"Beep! Beep!" Mr. Cameron honked his horn.
"Quack! Quack!" said Mother Duck.
"Cheep! Cheep!" said the ducklings.

But the cattle couldn't move –
because the road ahead was full of boys on bicycles,
going camping.

"Moo! Moo!" went the cattle.

"Beep! Beep!" Mr. Cameron honked his horn.

"Quack! Quack!" said Mother Duck.

"Cheep! Cheep!" said the ducklings.

But the boys couldn't move —
because a bus full of drummers on its
way to a concert was in their way.

"Brring! Brring!" the boys rang their bells.
"Moo! Moo!" went the cattle.
"Beep! Beep!" Mr. Cameron honked his horn.
"Quack! Quack!" said Mother Duck.
"Cheep! Cheep!" said the ducklings.

But the bus was stuck behind a man with
a motorcycle on his way to the river to fish.
　"Bang! Bang!" the drummers hit their drums.
　"Brring! Brring!" the boys rang their bells.
　"Moo! Moo!" went the cattle.
　"Beep! Beep!" Mr. Cameron honked his horn.
　"Quack! Quack!" said Mother Duck.
　"Cheep! Cheep!" said the ducklings.

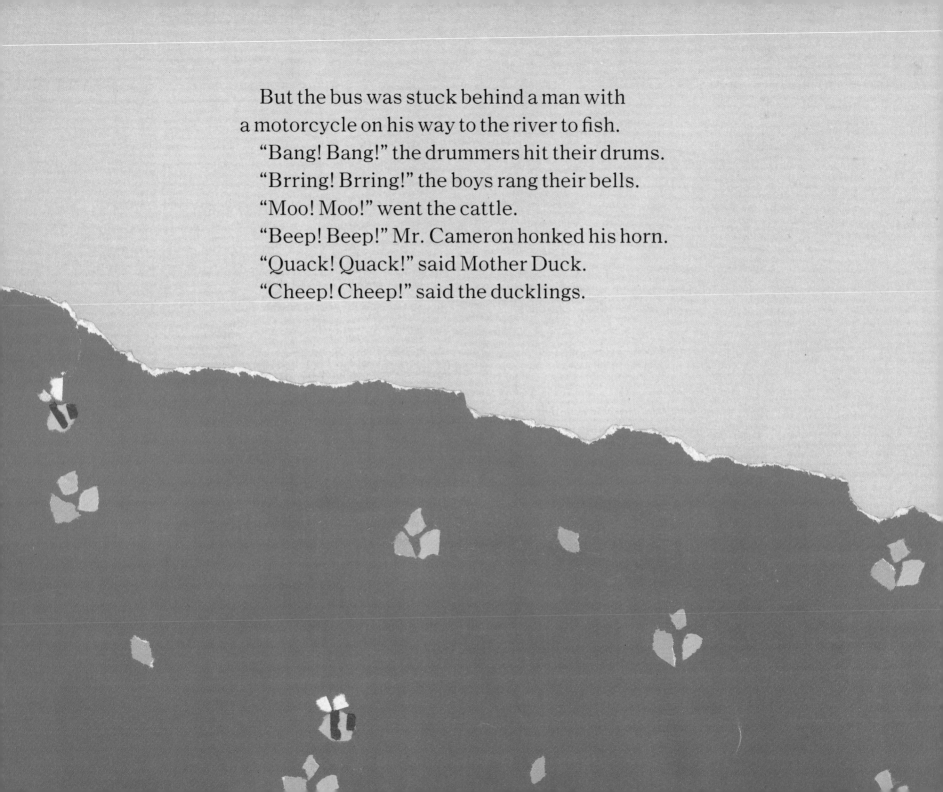

But the man on the motorcycle couldn't move
because he couldn't get past a flock of bleating
sheep which had strayed from the hill.

The sheep didn't know which way to go without
the help of Mr. MacGregor's sheepdog, Shep.

And Shep was waiting for his master to finish
his breakfast.

Mr. MacGregor had eaten his porridge and was waiting for Mrs. MacGregor to cook him an egg before he started work.

Mrs. MacGregor was waiting for Jamie, their son, to bring the egg from the little brown hen who lived in the hencoop behind the cottage.

But the little brown hen wouldn't lay an egg
unless Jamie gave her some corn—
and there was no more corn until Mr. Cameron
came to deliver it.

Jamie looked down the road and saw the long line stretching back to Mr. Cameron's truck.

He grabbed a bucket and ran down the hill.

"Please Mr. Cameron," he panted, "may I have a little corn to feed the hen until you reach the cottage?"

"Yes, Jamie, of course you may," said Mr. Cameron.

And Jamie took it up to the little brown hen as fast as he could.

"Cluck! Cluck!" She was so pleased that she laid
the egg that was keeping everyone waiting.

Jamie took it to his mother.

His mother cooked it for his father.

His father ate it and left the cottage, whistling to Shep.

"Woof! Woof! Baa! Baa!" Shep drove the sheep back to the hillside.

"Vroom! Vroom!" the man on the motorcycle went on his way to the river.

"Bang! Bang!" the bus full of drummers drove off to the concert.

"Brring! Brring!" the boys pedaled away towards their campsite.

"Moo! Moo!" the cattle went along the road to their grazing ground.

Mr. Cameron delivered the rest of the corn to the little brown hen . . .

. . . and Mother Duck and her ducklings could swim in the pond at last.
"Quack! Quack!"
"Cheep! Cheep!"